Peace at Last

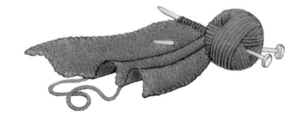

First published 1980 by Macmillan Children's Books
This revised edition published 2007 by Macmillan Children's Books
a division of Macmillan Publishers Limited
20 New Wharf Road, London N1 9RR
Basingstoke and Oxford
Associated companies throughout the world
www.panmacmillan.com

ISBN: 978-0-230-53241-0

3 5 7 9 8 6 4 2

A CIP catalogue record is available for this book from the British Library.

Printed in China

Peace at Last

Jill Murphy

MACMILLAN CHILDREN'S BOOKS

The hour was late.

Mr Bear was tired,
Mrs Bear was tired
and
Baby Bear was tired . . .

. . . so they all went to bed.

Mrs Bear fell asleep.
Mr Bear didn't.

Mrs Bear began to snore.
"SNORE," went Mrs Bear,
"SNORE, SNORE, SNORE."
"Oh NO!" said Mr Bear,
"I can't stand THIS."
So he got up and went to
sleep in Baby Bear's room.

Baby Bear was not asleep either.
He was lying in bed pretending
to be an aeroplane.
"NYAAOW!" went Baby Bear,
"NYAAOW! NYAAOW!"
"Oh NO!" said Mr Bear,
"I can't stand THIS."
So he got up
and went to sleep in the living room.

TICK-TOCK . . . went the living room
clock . . . TICK-TOCK, TICK-TOCK.
CUCKOO! CUCKOO!
"Oh NO!" said Mr Bear,
"I can't stand THIS!"
So he went off to sleep in the kitchen.

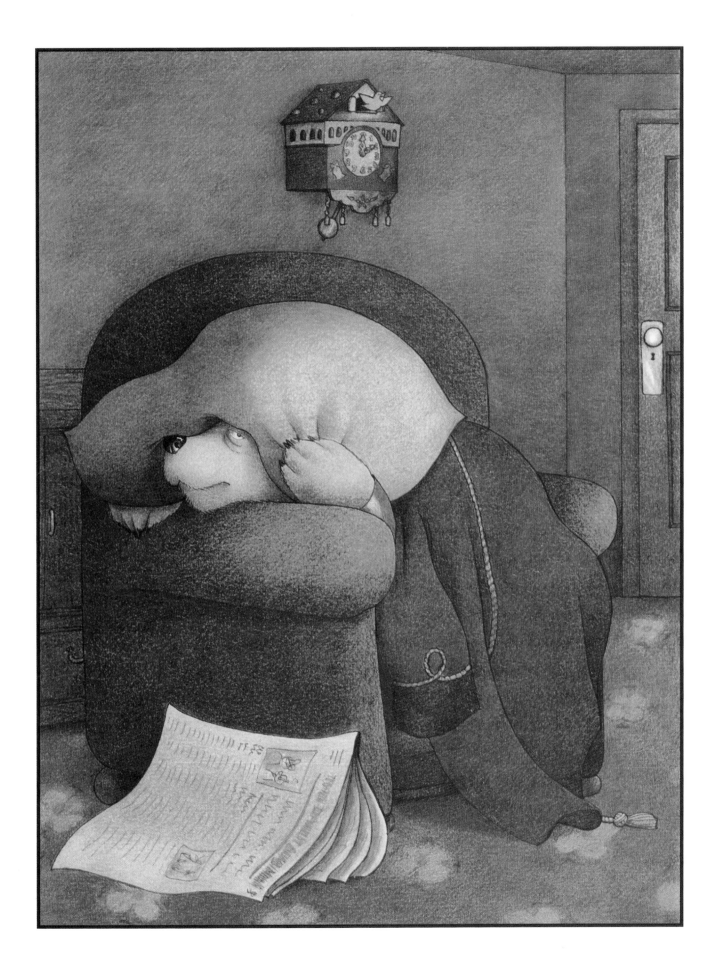

DRIP, DRIP . . . went the leaky
kitchen tap.
HMMMMMMMMMM . . .
went the refrigerator.
"Oh NO," said Mr Bear,
"I can't stand THIS."
So he got up
and went to sleep in the garden.

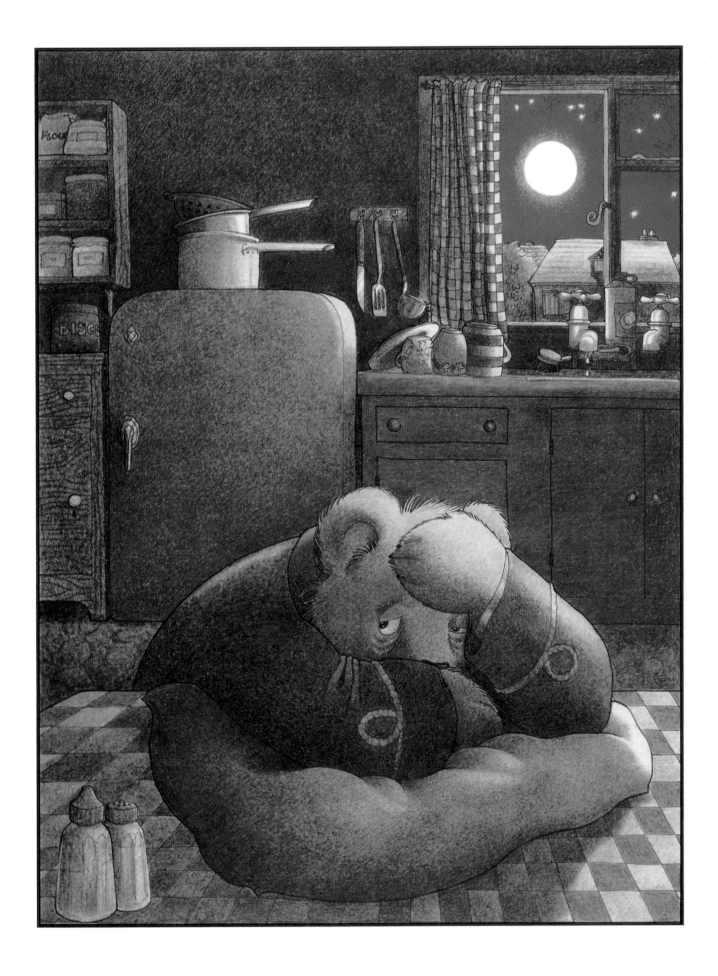

Well, you would not believe
what noises there are in
the garden at night.
"TOO-WHIT-TOO-WHOO!"
went the owl.
"SNUFFLE, SNUFFLE,"
went the hedgehog.
"MIAAAOW!" sang the cats
on the wall.
"Oh NO!" said Mr Bear,
"I can't stand THIS."
So he went off to sleep in the car.

It was cold in the car and
uncomfortable, but Mr Bear
was so tired that he didn't notice.
He was just falling asleep when
all the birds started to sing and
the sun peeped in at the window.
"TWEET TWEET!" went the birds.
SHINE, SHINE . . . went the sun.
"Oh NO!" said Mr Bear,
"I can't stand THIS."
So he got up and went back
into the house.

In the house, Baby Bear was
fast asleep, and Mrs Bear
had turned over and wasn't
snoring any more.
Mr Bear got into bed and
closed his eyes.
"Peace at last," he said to himself.

BRRRRRRRRRRRRRRR! went the
alarm clock, BRRRRRRR!
Mrs Bear sat up and rubbed her eyes.
"Good morning, dear," she said.
"Did you sleep well?"
"Not VERY well, dear," yawned
Mr Bear.
"Never mind," said Mrs Bear.
"I'll bring you a nice cup of tea."

And she did.